In
1935 if you wanted to
read a good book, you needed
either a lot of money or a library card.
Cheap paperbacks were available, but their
poor production generally mirrored the quality
between the covers. One weekend that year,
Allen Lane, Managing Director of The Bodley Head,
having spent the weekend visiting Agatha Christie,
found himself on a platform at Exeter station trying to
find something to read for his journey back to London.
He was appalled by the quality of the material he had to
choose from. Everything that Allen Lane achieved from that
day until his death in 1970 was based on a passionate belief
in the existence of 'a vast reading public for *intelligent*
books at a low price'. The result of his momentous vision
was the birth not only of Penguin, but of the 'paperback
revolution'. Quality writing became available for the price of
a packet of cigarettes, literature became a mass medium
for the first time, a nation of book-borrowers became a
nation of book-buyers – and the very concept of book
publishing was changed for ever. Those founding
principles – of quality and value, with an overarching
belief in the fundamental importance of reading –
have guided everything the company has
done since 1935. Sir Allen Lane's
pioneering spirit is still very much alive
at Penguin in 2005. Here's to
the next 70 years!

MORE THAN A BUSINESS

'We decided it was time to end the almost customary half-hearted manner in which cheap editions were produced – as though the only people who could possibly want cheap editions must belong to a lower order of intelligence. We, however, believed in the existence in this country of a vast reading public for intelligent books at a low price, and staked everything on it'
Sir Allen Lane, 1902–1970

'The Penguin Books are splendid value for sixpence, so splendid that if other publishers had any sense they would combine against them and suppress them'
George Orwell

'More than a business … a national cultural asset'
Guardian

'When you look at the whole Penguin achievement you know that it constitutes, in action, one of the more democratic successes of our recent social history'
Richard Hoggart

The Queen in Hell Close

SUE TOWNSEND

PENGUIN BOOKS

PENGUIN BOOKS

Published by the Penguin Group
Penguin Books Ltd, 80 Strand, London WC2R ORL, England
Penguin Group (USA) Inc., 375 Hudson Street, New York, New York 10014, USA
Penguin Group (Canada), 10 Alcorn Avenue, Toronto, Ontario, Canada M4V 3B2
(a division of Pearson Penguin Canada Inc.)
Penguin Ireland, 25 St Stephen's Green, Dublin 2, Ireland
(a division of Penguin Books Ltd)
Penguin Group (Australia), 250 Camberwell Road, Camberwell, Victoria 3124,
Australia (a division of Pearson Australia Group Pty Ltd)
Penguin Books India Pvt Ltd, 11 Community Centre,
Panchsheel Park, New Delhi – 110 017, India
Penguin Group (NZ), cnr Airborne and Rosedale Roads, Albany,
Auckland 1310, New Zealand (a division of Pearson New Zealand Ltd)
Penguin Books (South Africa) (Pty) Ltd, 24 Sturdee Avenue,
Rosebank 2196, South Africa

Penguin Books Ltd, Registered Offices: 80 Strand, London WC2R ORL, England

www.penguin.com

The Queen and I first published in Great Britain by Methuen 1992
First published in Penguin Books 2002
First published as a Pocket Penguin 2005

1

Copyright © Sue Townsend, 1992
All rights reserved

The moral right of the author has been asserted

Set in 11/13pt Monotype Dante
Typeset by Palimpsest Book Production Limited
Polmont, Stirlingshire
Printed in England by Clays Ltd, St Ives plc

The Briefcase Was Bare

The Queen was eating cornflakes in front of the television. A single cornflake fell from her mouth and landed on the carpet. Harris immediately licked it up.

The Queen said, 'What an absolute *slob* I'm becoming, Harris.' Her attention was then taken by a shouting match that had erupted in the TV-am studio. Jack Barker and the (usually genial) presenter of the programme were arguing about the health of the pound.

The presenter said, 'But, Mr Barker, the pound is desperately weak. It fell a long way last night.' She fixed him with a beady glance.

Really, thought the Queen. She makes it sound as though the pound had attempted a suicide jump from a tall building.

Jack smiled reassuringly: 'But, thanks to the measures we have taken, the pound is now rallying and is expected to hold its own.'

The Queen imagined the pound languishing in a hospital bed hooked up to monitors and drips, surrounded by anxious doctors and financial advisers.

The presenter turned to the camera and said, 'And now, the weather,' and the Queen went into the kitchen to wash her bowl and spoon.

*

Later that morning, there was a violent row in the street between Violet Toby and Beverley Threadgold.

Beverley wanted to know why she hadn't been woken up to officiate at her sister's confinement. Horrible wounding words were exchanged between the two women. Violet accused Beverley of neglecting Marilyn during her pregnancy. 'When was the last time you were inside your sister's stinking house?' bellowed Violet.

The Queen stood behind her closed front door and listened to the row. Both antagonists were shouting from their respective front gates. It wasn't difficult to hear what they were saying, both had foghorn voices when roused. Residents of Hell Close came out of their houses to enjoy the confrontation – it was unusual to have a shouting match in the spring. The long summer holiday was the traditional time – when the days were hot and the kids fell out and the mothers were irritable and longing for the first day of term.

To her alarm, the Queen heard her name mentioned. Beverley shouted, 'You just wanted to get in with the Queen.'

Violet shouted, 'I ain't no snob. I chose 'er because she were awake an' she don't panic. *Unlike* you, Beverley Threadgold, 'oo can't stand the sight of blood!'

The Queen came away from the door, not wishing to hear any more references to herself. It was true, she did keep a tight grip on herself. Would she go to her grave without experiencing an emotional breakdown? Was it better for one to hang onto the dictates of one's upbringing: good manners, control and self-discipline, or to behave how one *felt* and scream in the street like a demented harridan?

Once, when she was thirteen, she had belched at a dinner for the Hungarian Ambassador – an audible belch that was diplomatically ignored by the other distinguished diners. She had dismissed the belch to Crawfie, saying, 'Oh well, it's better out than in.'

Crawfie had said, 'No, no, no, Lilibet, it is always, always better *in* than out.'

What must it feel like to open one's mouth and *scream*? The Queen stood over the washing-up bowl and gave a tiny, experimental scream. To her ears, it sounded like a hinge needing oil. She tried again. 'Aaaaargh!' Quite satisfactory. And again, 'Aaaaaaaarggh!!!!' Her throat opened wide and the Queen could feel the scream travel up her lungs, overflow her windpipe and roar out of her mouth like a British lion. The scream woke Philip, it brought people running to the Queen's front door. It caused Harris to lie low and flatten his ears, birds left the Queen's garden in a flapping panic, earthworms burrowed deeper.

The scream drew attention away from the row in the street and the man from the Department of Social Security paused before opening the Queen's gate and walking up the path. What on earth was going on *now*? Was the Queen being murdered? Had he brought the correct forms for a Funeral Claim?

The Queen opened the front door and assured her neighbours that she was perfectly well. She had trodden on a drawing pin in her stockinged feet. All eyes looked down. The Queen was wearing sturdy green wellingtons.

The man from the DSS pushed through the sceptical crowd and introduced himself: 'I'm David Dorkin, from the DSS. I've come to sort out your benefit.'

The Queen led him into the living room and invited him to sit on the Napoleonic sofa. She advised him to avoid the join where the six inch nails had been hammered in. Dorkin opened his metal briefcase and started to take out his forms and lay them on the lid. He was nervous: who wouldn't be? He couldn't find his pen, and the Queen went to her desk and handed him a heavy gold fountain pen, worth twice his annual salary. Dorkin said, 'I can't use a fountain pen!' He had taken the top off and seen the encrustation of small jewels around the nib. It was too much of a responsibility, he felt. What if he damaged it? There could be a huge insurance claim. He handed the pen back to the Queen, took a deep breath, searched in his beige anorak and located his own rollerball. With a pen in his hand he felt more in command of himself. He declined coffee.

'I'd like your husband to be present at this interview,' said Dorkin.

'My husband is unwell,' said the Queen. 'He has been unwell since we moved in.'

'Since your relocation?' said Dorkin.

'Since we *moved in*,' repeated the Queen.

The rollerball rolled over the page of Dorkin's reporter's notebook.

'And what is the current situation regarding your personal finances?'

'We are penniless. I have been forced to borrow from my mother; but now my mother is also penniless. As is my entire family. I have been forced to rely on the charity of neighbours. But I cannot continue to do so. My neighbours are . . .' The Queen paused.

'Socially disadvantaged?' supplied Dorkin.

'No, they are *poor*,' said the Queen. 'They, like me, lack money. I would like you, Mr Dorkin, to give me some money – today, please. I have no food, no heat and when the electricity goes, I will have no light.'

'When your claim is processed and approved, you will receive a giro through the post,' said Dorkin.

As it was Friday the Queen had expected this young man with the prominent Adam's apple simply to take banknotes from out of his briefcase and hand them over to her. All of her family were under a similar misapprehension, which was why they had been spending that week with such abandon. She tried once again to explain to Dorkin that she needed the money immediately; there was nothing in the refrigerator, the cupboards were bare.

Right on cue, Prince Philip shuffled into the room, bleating that he'd had no breakfast, demanding to know where his contact lenses were, complaining of the cold.

Dorkin was shocked at Philip's disintegration: seen on television before the election, he had appeared to be a vigorous man, immaculately dressed, with a healthy pink complexion and an arrogant bearing. Dorkin could hardly bring himself to look at the broken wreck in front of him. It was like finding your own father lying drunk in a gutter. The Queen pacified Philip with the promise of coffee, led him to the foot of the stairs and urged him back to bed.

When she re-entered the living room, she saw that David Dorkin had started to fill in a form. Was this the previously mentioned Claim Form? If so, it must be completed at once. Philip and Harris must be fed. She had always had a small appetite; she would manage. But the man and the dog were helpless and entirely dependent upon her ability to navigate a course through the murky waters of the DSS.

When the form was completed, the Queen asked when she would receive the giro. 'It could be a week, though we're short-staffed, so . . .' Dorkin's voice trailed off.

'So?'

'It could be longer; perhaps nine, ten days.'

'But how can we exist without food for ten days? You surely won't allow us to *starve*?' said the Queen to the young man. Dorkin grudgingly admitted that starvation was not official policy. 'There is,' he said, 'such a thing as an Emergency Payment.'

'And how does one procure an Emergency Payment?' asked the Queen.

'You have to go to the DSS office, in person,' he said. He warned her that even as he spoke the queue would be out of the door, but the Queen already had her coat on. She simply couldn't keep borrowing from the neighbours. She tied a headscarf around her head. As she had no money, she would have to walk into town.

The Gamblers

Fitzroy Toussaint was surprised to find that his mother was not at home. He always called on Fridays at 1 pm and she was usually on the doorstep, waiting for him – whatever the weather. He let himself into her bungalow with a key. Fitzroy was grateful he didn't have to live in the Close himself any more. Once he had taken his 'A' levels he had got the hell out and gone to live in the suburbs. Christ, it was cold! He went through the narrow hall to the kitchen. Good, at least she had plenty of food; the shelves in her high cupboard were well stocked. So why was she so *thin?* She was wasting away, her legs and arms were like sticks, no, twigs.

As usual, the interior of the bungalow was immaculate, the dishcloth was folded into a square on the draining board. He looked into the bedroom and saw that the bed was made and that she had started to knit her Christmas presents for the grandchildren. He was cheered by this – her arthritis couldn't be any worse. He put his head around the living room door and saw a note tucked into the mirror over the cold fireplace.

'Fitzroy, I am next door, with the Queen Mother. Call round, she don't mind, I axed.'

The Queen Mother's door was slightly ajar. Fitzroy pushed it and was met by a gust of hot air. He waited and heard his mother's voice raised in indignation, telling one of her family stories.

'That woman was *evil*, I tell you, to run off and leave her children . . .'

He heard the Queen Mother's voice trying, and eventually succeeding in cutting in. 'Wallis Simpson was evil too, I'm convinced of it. I will never forgive her for what she did to poor David. It was a dreadful time for us all. Abdication! It was so shaming. He knew my husband, George, didn't want to be King – who would, with a stammer like his? All those speeches, it was torture for him – and me.'

Fitzroy heard his mother shouting the Queen Mother down. 'An' this is another wicked woman! Me Aunt Matilda. Man, that woman was crazy for the drink. See, if you look careful you can see the bottle in her hand.'

Fitzroy knocked on the living room door, walked in and found two old ladies, each looking through her own family photograph album. Both too old to care what other people thought of them, both relishing the airing of family secrets.

Fitzroy saw the pleasure on his mother's face when she saw him. He also saw the slight flicker of fear on the Queen Mother's face. Did she think he was going to rob her? Did the suit and the Filofax he was carrying under his arm count for nothing?

'Hello, Mum,' he said, and was only a little surprised when both women said, 'Hello, Fitzroy.'

His mother bombarded him with questions as usual. How was his chest? Was he still working hard? Was he cooking himself proper meals? Had he heard from Troy?

Why had he shaved off his moustache? It was cold, was he wearing a vest? Had he visited Jethroe's grave? Did he want a hot drink?

The Queen Mother insisted that they must take tea with her. She got up from her chair with great difficulty, Fitzroy noticed. He offered her his hand and she leaned heavily against him.

'Sit down, woman!' shouted Philomena. 'Talk to me son. I hain't as old as you. I'll make the tea.'

She stomped off into the kitchen as though it were her own house. The Queen Mother sat down and asked Fitzroy if he was interested in horses. Fitzroy wondered if this was a trap. He had promised his mother that he would never gamble. On his eighteenth birthday she had made him swear on the Bible that he would never set foot inside a bookie's shop. He had kept his promise.

When he was twenty-one, he had opened a telephone account with Jack Johnson, Turf Accountant. His winnings were sent straight into his bank account but, like the Queen Mother, he had never set foot inside a bookie's shop. He lowered his voice and moved nearer to the Queen Mother.

'Yeah, I'm interested.'

'In form?'

'Yeah, in form.'

'Who trained my grandson's horse, Sea Swell?'

Fitzroy answered at once, 'Nick Gaselee, for the Duke of Gloucester Memorial Trophy. Prince Charles finished fourth.'

'Yes, I lost twenty-five pounds.'

The Queen Mother pulled from her corsage a five

pound note she had been concealing from her daughter and handed it to Fitzroy.

'Sea Mist – Kempton Park, two o'clock,' she said, with her eye on the kitchen door.

'To win?'

'Oh yes, it's a cert, the going's soft, he likes it soft.'

Fitzroy took a mobile telephone from the inside pocket of his Paul Smith jacket. He pressed the buttons and placed the Queen Mother's bet. And, just to be friendly, he put twenty-five pounds on Sea Mist himself. They swapped gambling stories until Philomena came in with the tea tray and they talked about Fitzroy's job. He was an insolvency accountant, currently bringing a chain of shoe shops to a peaceful end. He promised to get the Queen Mother a pair of wide-fitting brocade house slippers – at a discount.

At 2.15 Fitzroy's telephone rang. Philomena was washing up noisily in the kitchen. 'Yeah?' he said, looking at the Queen Mother. 'Wellwotjano! You've won yourself a tidy amount.'

The Queen Mother's eyes glittered greedily.

'Right,' she whispered. 'Nectarine – Kempton Park; two-thirty. Twenty pounds each way.'

It made him late getting back to the office but he waited until 2.35, when the phone rang again. This time his mother was back in the room so all he did was show the Queen Mother his downturned thumb. She understood at once.

Philomena collected up her photograph albums and ordered the Queen Mother to have a nap. She was tired herself and needed to sleep.

Fitzroy saw his mother to her front door and handed her a small plastic bag full of fifty pence coins. 'For the gas meter,' he said. 'Use them.' He walked to his Ford Sierra with an extra spring in his step, pleased with his winnings and glad that his mother had a friend. Man, it took a weight off his shoulders. He pressed a button on his key ring and a mysterious electronic process caused the door locks to pop up in unison. He waved goodbye to the two old ladies waving from their respective front windows and reversed towards the barrier. He didn't like meeting the police head on. Never had.

The Long Walk

Harris was playing in the street with the Pack. The Queen stood on her doorstep calling him in, but he refused to come. She ran out into the street, shouting his name angrily. A gang of children joined in the chase. What a scruffy bunch they were, thought the Queen. Then she noticed that running amongst them, like feral animals, were her own grandchildren, William and Harry. Harris ran and hid under a wrecked and burnt out Renault car that stood at the kerb. The Queen lured him out with a polo mint she'd found in the pocket of her waxed coat, then she thrashed him with his lead. But it was a gentle thrashing.

Harris allowed the lead to be slipped over his head and the Queen set off to walk the three miles into town. As she approached the barrier, she saw that PC Ludlow was on duty, checking the licence of a handsome and smartly dressed black man who was behind the wheel of a Ford Sierra.

When the car had reversed rapidly out of Hell Close, she went up to Ludlow and demanded to know why he had told such shocking lies in court. PC Ludlow had dreaded this moment. He hadn't slept properly for three nights – guilt had kept him awake. He had listened to the World Service on his clock radio until the early hours, trying to blot out the memory of the crime he had committed. Perjury was a serious offence; he could lose his job. It was unlikely, but you never knew nowadays.

Inspector Holyland had told him what to say and he had said it, word for word. He hadn't expected to be believed. 'Kill the pig!' He had expected the magistrates and the court and the public gallery to burst into laughter at the thought of the Prince of Wales uttering these clichéd words, but he was wearing his uniform, he represented Law and Order and Truth; and Inspector Holyland had backed him up, although he hadn't been on the scene at the time.

The Queen repeated, 'Why did you tell those lies about my son?' Ludlow said, 'Those were the facts as I saw them, at the time.' Harris was sniffing around the bottom of his trousers. Ludlow moved his feet and Harris, interpreting this as an aggressive gesture, sank his teeth into a regulation police sock, piercing the skin below. In Ludlow's opinion, the Queen took an unnecessarily long time in pulling Harris away from his left ankle. There was a form to fill in before she was allowed to leave Hell Close.

Name	Elizabeth Windsor
Address	9 Hell Close
Time	2.45 pm
Destination	DSS Middleton
Method of transport	Walking
Estimated time of return	6 pm

Ludlow lifted the barrier and she walked through.

A bogus beast followed her, keeping his distance.

Surely she wasn't going to *walk* into town? He'd got new shoes on. His feet would be in tatters. He was festooned in corn plasters as it was. He was sick of being in plain clothes. He longed for the comfort of his old panda car. His name was Colin Lightfoot, his duty was to shadow the Queen and report back to Inspector Holyland.

The Queen was quite enjoying the walk, though she would have preferred to be on Holkham Beach, near Sandringham – or striding through the heather at Balmoral. But at least she was out of Hell Close and getting some exercise. Harris hated it. The pavements were hard on his feet and his little legs could hardly keep up with the Queen's vigorous pace.

They were walking alongside the dual carriageway that connected the Flowers Estate to the town. The Queen had visited the town before; she had opened a hospital, visited a hosiery and light engineering factory in the morning and, after lunch in the Town Hall, had visited an institution for the elderly confused in the after- noon, where she had made excruciatingly embarrassing conversation with the residents. One old, dribbling man was convinced that she was his mother and that it was 1941 and that he was still in the Catering Corps. On her way back to the Royal Train, she had called in at a proba- tion hostel where she was given a tour of the gleaming dormitories and the freshly painted ping-pong room. A few presentable probationers had been allowed to look on while the daughter of the Director of Social Services had given her a bunch of spring flowers. She wondered now where the other, probably less presentable, proba- tioners had been kept.

It began to rain; a steady remorseless sheet of water. She pulled her headscarf lower, over her forehead, and strode on. The bogus beast behind her cursed and swore and shook his fist at the heavens and, as if to taunt him, a police car drove by, the uniformed occupants looking warm and smug as they conveyed Mr Christmas to Tulip Street Police Station.

She looked at her watch and quickened her step. Mr Dorkin had told her that the office closed at 5.30. He had written down the address on a sheet of paper. The Queen took the folded sheet from her pocket. The only legible words were 'DSS Office'. The remaining address was completely illegible, rain had run into her pocket and obliterated everything below the fold of the paper.

Harris tried to match the Queen's more urgent pace to his own, but after a few minutes he had had enough and refused to go on. He *knew* he should have worn his raincoat. He had stood under the coat rack in the hall. He had barked and indicated that he would like to be strapped into his little coat, but *she* was in too much of a hurry to notice *him*, wasn't she? Oh yes, hadn't got a moment now to feed him and tell him that he was her favourite. And what *was* it with all this physical *violence?* A beating a day – at least. If she wasn't careful . . . he knew about the RSPCA. And, another thing, he had *serious* fleas. The Queen yanked on Harris's lead, but he refused to budge. She tried dragging him along but he sat down and dug his paws in. A bedraggled passer-by said, 'You'll have the skin off that dog's arse.'

The Queen replied, 'I'll have the skin off that dog's *back* if he doesn't move.' She pushed Harris with her foot and he yelped as though in agony and lay on his back feigning death. Through a slit in one eye, he watched as the Queen bent over him, her eyes full of concern and guilt. He felt himself being lifted up and cradled in her arms.

Their journey continued along the dual carriageway towards the town where the pavements were not paved with gold – they were hardly paved at all. The Council were investing their money in buying a windswept thousand-acre site on the outskirts of the town where they planned to build a theme park: a zoo without animals. Instead of the mess and the smell and the necessity to feed real wild animals, the Council had been persuaded by a private company to build a series of huge windowless edifices. Inside, electronic imagery and sophisticated sound systems were to replicate the continents of the world and their indigenous animals. It was Virtual Reality on a huge scale. Millions of goggling visitors were expected to visit the windswept site from all over Britain. A five hundred bed hotel was to be built to accommodate them. The narrow minor roads leading to the site were to be widened slightly. They had hoped that Prince Philip (in his capacity as President of the World Wildlife Fund, rather than his other well-known role as killer of small birds and animals) would open the electronic zoo for them.

When the Queen reached the town centre, she rested on a bench and put Harris on his feet. He lifted his leg and urinated against an overflowing litter bin. The Queen was reminded of Niagara Falls, the flow of which, unlike Harris, could be switched off at will.

A man was sitting next to the Queen. He had a raw, recently broken nose. He was drinking out of a brown bottle. After each drink he drew a filthy hand across his mouth, as if hiding the evidence. His shoes were of the type worn by bandleaders between the wars. Harris's urine trickled towards these shoes and the man drew his feet onto the bench in a decorous movement, like a young girl avoiding a strolling spider.

The Queen apologized for Harris's behaviour.

'Och, the wee dog canna help it,' said the man, his voice hoarse from violent shouting in the small hours. 'An' let's face it, missus, he's too wee to climb onto a lavatory seat.'

The man laughed and choked at his joke and when he saw that the Queen was not laughing, he prodded her and said, 'Aw, c'mon, lassie, let yourself go. You've got a face on you like a wet Sunday in Aberdeen.'

The Queen showed her teeth briefly and the man was pacified.

He said, 'D'you know who you look like? I'll tell you. You look like that woman who impersonates the Queen. You do, you do, you look like her – wassaname? You know the one. You look *more* like her than she does. You do. You do. You could make a *fortune*. You shid do it, you shid. You shid do it. You know who *I've* been taken for?'

The Queen looked at his broken veined face. His tropical sunset eyes, his matted hair, his verdigris teeth.

'G'wan, guess who I'm took for?'

'I simply can't imagine,' said the Queen, turning her head away from his cidery breath.

'Hee, hee, hee,' laughed the man. 'Hee, hee, hee, that's verra guid. You sound jus' like her. *"Ai simplay carrnt eemaygin"*,' he mocked. 'Jus' like her, jus' like the Queen. You shid go on the clubs, you shid. *"Ai simplay carrnt eemaygin"*.' His laughter echoed around the town centre. He beat on his thighs with his fists. 'I mean, you're not tellin' me that her accent is *real*. It's not, it's not. It's not real. She sounds like a robot from *Doctor Who*. Doesn't she, missus? Doesn't she? Still, we're rid of her now. Guid riddance, I say. I'll drink to that. I'll drink to that. Who's in charge now?'

'Jack Barker,' said the Queen, trying to flatten her vowels.

'Tee hee, hee. *Jek Barker*. You're a scream, missus,' said the Republican. 'You are, you are, you are.'

He stood up and swayed in front of the Queen. She noticed that he was not wearing socks. His trouser hems had fallen down; overlocking threads trailed behind him. If ever asked by a style magazine journalist to explain how he chose each day's wardrobe, he would have to say in all honesty that he threw his clothes on in the morning and continued to wear them day and night until many months later when they were removed by men wearing rubber gloves, overalls and face masks.

'G'wan, who do I remind you of?' He struck what he perceived to be an artistic pose. One finger on his chin, and his head turned to display his wrecked profile.

The Queen shook her head; she didn't know.

'The Duke,' shouted the dissolute one. He saw that the Queen was not familiar with the name. 'Prince

Philip. I'm a dead ringer for him; everybody says, everybody. Can you not see it? Can you not?'

The Queen eventually admitted that perhaps there was a 'slight resemblance'. He drank the bottle dry, then shook it and steered two brown drops into his gaping mouth. He shook it again, inverted it against his mouth, waited, got angry when nothing appeared and banged his teeth on the rim.

'You wouldn't have the price of a Big Mac, would you missus?' he asked.

'No,' said the Queen, placing the cider bottle against the litter bin. 'I do not have a penny.'

'Och, that's what they all say, though not in such a classy accent.'

The Queen asked him for directions to the DSS office. He offered to escort the Queen to the door, but she declined graciously. As she waited for the green man to give her permission to cross the road, she heard the grimy one shout, 'Jeanette Charles! That's her, that's her, that's the one. You're a dead ringer for her. A fortune! A fortune!'

The Queen joined the queue outside the DSS office. A girl in unmemorable clothes gave her a numbered disc – thirty-nine. She stood behind number thirty-eight and was soon joined by forty. Those in the queue with watches looked at them, frequently. Those without asked the time, often.

Time, invisible and invincible, fled by, mocking those waiting outside. Would they be seen? There were twenty-five minutes left. They did mathematical calculations inside their heads. Little children stood stoically holding onto the pushchairs of their younger siblings.

The rush hour traffic jerked by, three feet away, sending fumes directly into the lungs of the occupants of the pushchairs.

Harris coughed and strained on his lead.

The queue shuffled in until the Queen was sufficiently far forward to be able to see inside the large room where a menacing clock with black hands and a hurrying second hand told her that it was twelve minutes past five. A baby began to cry and was given an unopened packet of crisps to suck.

''S no good givin' him a actual *crisp*, they're salt and vinegar,' said the young mother – number thirty-eight. ''E don't like salt 'n' vinegar.'

The Queen nodded, reluctant to open her mouth and advertise her class. Her accent was proving to be rather a bother. Should she try to modify it? And her grammar was a nuisance. Should she throw in a few double negatives? It was terribly difficult to work out where she *belonged* any more – except as a number between thirty-eight and forty.

As the hands of the clock moved towards 5.30, the queue started to panic and surge towards the counters where claimants were seated, pleading their cases through grilles set into sheets of safety glass.

Words of supplication, anger and desperation passed one way through the screen from the waiting room to the office. In the other direction passed words pertaining to regulations, explanations and refusal. A man stood up and banged on the screen, 'I need some money – now,' he shouted. 'I can't go home without some money. We've got nowt.'

The clerk sat impassively and watched a security guard lead the man away.

'Thirty-six,' said the clerk. 'Thirty-seven,' said another.

A third clerk left her desk and gathered her papers and her boxed pen and pencil set together. She slung the strap of her bag over her shoulder and prepared to leave.

The Queen left her place in the queue and said through the grille, 'Excuse me, but at what time do you leave your work?'

The clerk said reluctantly, 'Half past five.'

'Then you have five minutes left,' said the Queen. 'Perhaps your watch is rather fast.'

The clerk resumed her seat and said, 'Thirty-eight.' The Queen rejoined the queue, who were pleased at the small victory. Behind her, forty said, 'Good show, ma'am.' He came closer and said out of the side of his mouth, 'I had the honour to serve in your regiment, Welsh Guards. Saw action in the Falklands, Bluff Cove. Honourable discharge. Nerves gone to pot.'

'A bad show,' said the Queen, who was the former Colonel-in-Chief of thirty-eight regiments and the Captain General of seven others.

Her number was called by a pleasant-looking Asian youth. The Queen had two minutes in which to state her case and leave with bus fare, food money and coins for the meters. 'It's impossible,' smiled the youth, after she had answered that no, she had no documentation to prove who she was and where she lived.

'To get an Emergency Payment, we need proof; a pension book? A gas bill?'

The Queen explained that she had not yet received her pension book. She had only been in her present accommodation for four days.

'And where did you live before?' asked the youth.

'At Buckingham Palace,' answered the Queen.

'Sure you did,' laughed the youth, looking at the Queen's coat covered in muddy paw prints, at her grimy nails, her wet straggling hair. Honest. He had heard all sorts of stories. He could write a book! Two books. Honest.

'And why were you living in Buckingham Palace?' he asked, raising his voice so that his fellow workers would be able to share the joke.

'Because I was the Queen,' said the Queen.

The youth pressed a buzzer under his counter and a security guard took the Queen's arm and led her and Harris out into the dark evening. She stood on the pavement, not knowing what to do or where to go for help. She tried all her pockets, searching for a coin for the telephone, though she knew perfectly well that her pockets were completely empty apart from a sheet of lavatory paper torn from a roll. She didn't know that it was possible to make a reverse charge call through the operator.

It was Friday night, the DSS would be closed for two days. They had money, she had none.

Dragging Harris behind her, she ran back into the office. The staff were wearing their coats. The clock said that it was five twenty-nine and thirty seconds. Claimants were being escorted from the room. The Queen noticed that number thirty-eight had a five pound note in her hand and was talking to her baby:

telling the child that she was going to buy milk and bread and nappies. Forty was refusing to leave: 'I was at Bluff Cove,' he was shouting.

The Queen picked Harris up and put him under her arm. 'My dog is starving,' she announced to the room.

Clerk number two lived with her mother, three dogs and five cats. She had wanted to be a vet but couldn't get the 'A' levels. She looked at Harris, who lay languidly in the Queen's arms as though he were in the last stages of malnutrition. The clerk sat down behind her desk. She unbuttoned her coat, reached for a pen and invited the Queen to sit down. First she lectured the Queen on the responsibilities of dog ownership, saying, 'You shouldn't really keep a dog unless you're prepared to, well, *keep* it properly.'

Harris whimpered pitifully and allowed his ears to droop. The clerk continued her lecture. 'He looks in very bad condition. I'm going to give you enough for a couple of tins of dog food and some conditioning tablets – Bob Martin's are good.'

The Queen took the money, signed the receipt and left the office. She thanked God that the English were a nation of dog lovers.

A Bag of Bones

The bogus beast followed her. As she left the office, he prayed that she was not planning to walk home. His feet were raw lumps of meat. He couldn't wait to take his shoes off. The Queen clutched the three pound coins tightly in her hand. How much was a loaf of bread? A pound of potatoes? A jar of coffee? She had no intention of buying dog food or conditioning tablets for Harris.

Crawfie used to make broth whenever the Queen was ill as a child. The Queen remembered that bones were involved. She passed a butcher's shop. A man in a white coat and striped apron was scrubbing the shelves in the display cabinet. Small bunches of plastic parsley were piled up on the shop counter, waiting to be replaced in order to beautify the shelves. The Queen tied Harris up outside and pushed the door open.

'We're closed,' said the butcher.

'Could you sell me some bones?' asked the Queen.

'I'm closed,' he said.

The Queen pleaded, 'Please. They're for my dog.'

The butcher sighed, went out to the back and returned with a collection of gruesome bones which he slung onto the scales.

'Thirty pence,' he said, brusquely, wrapping them loosely in a sheet of paper. The Queen handed him a pound coin and he took the change from a bag of coins and handed it to her without a smile.

'May I have a carrier bag?' the Queen asked.

'No, not for thirty pence,' said the butcher.

'Oh well, thank you and goodnight,' said the Queen. She didn't know how much it would cost to buy a carrier. She couldn't risk spending perhaps twenty or thirty pence more.

The Queen said again, 'Goodnight.'

The butcher turned his back and began to place the plastic parsley around the edge of the display shelves.

The Queen said, 'Have I offended you in some way?'

The butcher said, 'Look, you've got your thirty pence worth, just close the door behind you.'

Before she could do as she was told, a well-dressed man came into the shop and said, 'I can see you're closed, but will you sell me three pounds of fillet steak?'

The butcher smiled and said, 'Certainly, sir, won't be a tick.'

The Queen took her bones and left. As she untied Harris, she watched the butcher through the window as he sliced fat slices of steak from a large lump of beef. He was now all jollity, like a butcher on a playing card.

Harris was maddened by the smell of the bones. He leapt up toward the parcel which was tucked under the Queen's arm. When they got to the bus stop, she threw a small knuckle bone onto the pavement and he attacked it ferociously, holding it in his front paws and tearing at the wisps of flesh with guttural, greedy sounds.

The bone was stripped bare by the time the bus arrived. The town centre was almost deserted. The

Queen dreaded the weekend ahead. How did one feed oneself, one's husband and one's dog on two pounds and ten pence, which was all she had, after paying her bus fare? She simply could not borrow any more. She would pray that her pension book came in the post tomorrow.

The Queen said, 'One to the Flowers Estate, please.'

She put sixty pence in the driver's black scoop bowl and waited for her ticket. The driver said, 'I want ninety pee. It's 'alf fare for the dog.'

The Queen was horrified, 'Surely not?'

'Dog's 'alf fare,' repeated the driver.

The Queen gave Harris a venomous look. For two pins, she'd make him run behind the bus. He'd been nothing but a nuisance all day. However, she paid up and, as instructed by the driver, carried Harris upstairs to the top deck. She counted and recounted her money, but always came to the same total: one pound and eighty pence. She closed her eyes and prayed for a miracle – of the loaves and fishes variety.

The Queen got off the bus and went into the Food-U-R – the supermarket that served the Flowers Estate. The manager and owner was Victor Berryman. He stood at the door greeting customers and watching out for shoplifters.

'Evening, madam. Settling in all right?'

The Queen smiled and nodded. 'Yes, finding one's way.'

'That's what I like to hear. Sorry to hear about your husband.'

'My husband?'

'Yes, I hear he's bad.'

'Bad?'

'Poorly, off his head.'

'He's depressed, certainly.'

'I know how he feels. I used to have a chain of these, you know. There were Food-U-Rs all over the East Midlands. Adverts on the telly. The hula girls? Food-U-R – a Paradise for Shoppers?' He sang the jingle and swayed his bulky hips.

> Food-U-R!
> A Paradise for Shoppers.
> Food-U-R!

'I tried to get the girls to go with the Polynesian theme – you know, grass skirts, garlands, but there was nothing but complaints.'

He looked bitterly towards the checkouts where two dumpy, middle-aged women were passing groceries in front of electronic scanners: 'Yes, I was once head of a dynasty, so I know how your husband feels – having it snatched away.'

The Queen scowled. 'My husband was not the head of the dynasty. I was.'

Victor Berryman snatched a Mars Bar from the inside jacket pocket of a departing boy, clipped him round the ear and kicked him out of the shop.

'Anyway, madam, if there's anything I can do to help,' said Victor, shaking his fist at the boy.

The Queen explained that she wished to make a broth.

'A brawth?' repeated Victor.

'A broth – a thin stew,' the Queen explained. 'I have the bones, what else does one need?'

Victor looked baffled, the kitchen was a place of mystery to him. All he knew was that cold ingredients were taken in and hot food came out, at more or less regular intervals. He called to one of the women at the checkout, 'Mrs Maundy, help this lady out, will you? I'll take over the till.'

Mrs Maundy gave the Queen a half curtsey and a wire basket and they promenaded up and down the aisles. The Queen bought one onion, two carrots, one turnip, one pound of potatoes, a large loaf of bread, a jar of strawberry jam (small) and two Oxo cubes.

Victor Berryman passed the Queen's groceries over the magic eye and said, 'One pound fifty-eight pence.'

'Oh dear.'

The Queen looked at the pound and eighty pence in her hand.

'I will have to put something back,' she said. 'I need fifty pence for the meter.'

Between them, they worked out that if she discarded one carrot and one Oxo cube, and swapped a large loaf for a small one . . .

The Queen left the shop carrying a Food-U-R bag. Victor held the door open for her and said he hoped he would see her again, perhaps she would recommend him to her family and, if she had a spare crest hanging around doing nothing, he'd be pleased to hang it up over the front door.

The Queen had been trained to ask questions, so, as

she untied Harris's lead from a concrete bollard, she asked Victor how he had lost his dynasty of Food-U-R stores.

'The Bank,' he answered as he checked the padlocks on the metal grilles that covered the windows. 'They hassled me to borrow money to expand. Then interest rates went up an' I couldn't make the payments. Serves me right, really, I lost the lot. The wife took it hard; house was sold, cars. Nobody wanted to buy this place on the Flowers Estate – who would, 'part from a maniac? We live above the shop now.' The Queen looked up and saw a woman whom she took to be Mrs Berryman, looking sadly out of an uncurtained window.

'Still,' said Victor, 'it's nothing to what *you've* lost, is it?'

The Queen, who had lost palaces, property, land, jewels, paintings, houses, a yacht, a plane, a train, over a thousand servants and billions of pounds, nodded her agreement.

Victor took out a comb and drew it across his bald head. 'Next time you're here, come up and see the wife. Have a cup of tea – she's always in; she's an agora-phobic.' The Queen looked up again, but the sad face at the window had gone.

Clutching her fifty pence coin in her hand, the Queen walked back to Hell Close. Behind her, keeping his distance, limped the bogus beast. If this is plain clothes duty, give me a uniform any day, he thought.

As the Queen let herself into her house, she heard a familiar cough. Margaret was there. Yes, there she sat, smoking and tapping ash into a coffee cup.

'Lilibet, you look absolutely ghastly! And what have you got in that horrid smelly plastic bag?'

'Bones, for our dinner.'

Margaret said: 'I've had the most appalling time this afternoon with a ghastly little man from the Social Security. He was unspeakably vile.'

They moved into the kitchen. The Queen half-filled a saucepan with water and threw the bones into it. Margaret watched intently as though the Queen were Paul Daniels about to perform a magic trick.

'Are you good at peeling potatoes, Margaret?'

'No, of course not, are you?'

'No, but one has to try.'

'Go ahead, try,' yawned Margaret. 'I'm going out to dinner tonight. I telephoned Bobo Criche-Hutchinson; he's got a house in the county. He's picking me up at 8.30.'

A scum formed on the saucepan, then the water boiled over and extinguished the gas flame. The Queen relit the gas ring and said, 'You know we aren't allowed to go out to dinner; we're still under curfew. You'd better ring Bobo and put him off. You haven't read Jack Barker's sheet of instructions, have you?'

'No, I tore it into pieces.'

'Better read mine,' said the Queen, as she hacked at a King Edward with a table knife. 'In my handbag.'

When she had finished reading, Margaret inserted another cigarette inside a holder and said, 'I'll kill myself.'

'That is one option,' said the Queen. 'But what would Crawfie think if you did?'

'Who cares *what* that evil old witch thinks about anything? Anyway, she's dead,' burst out Margaret.

'Not for me, she's not. She's with me at all times, Margaret.'

'She hated me,' said Margaret. 'She made no secret of it.'

'You were a hateful little girl, that's why. Bossy, arrogant and sly,' said the Queen. 'Crawfie said you'd make a mess of your life and she was right – you have.'

After half an hour of silence, the Queen apologized for her outburst. She explained that Hell Close had that effect on one. One got used to speaking one's mind. It was inconvenient at times, but one felt strangely *good* afterwards.

Margaret went into the living room to telephone Bobo Criche-Hutchinson, leaving the Queen to throw the root vegetables and the Oxo cube into the saucepan. Mrs Maundy had told her that broth has to simmer on a low heat for hours – 'to draw the goodness out' – but the Queen was ravenous, she needed to eat *now*, at once. Something tasty and filling and sweet. She reached for the bread and jam and made herself a pile of sandwiches. She ate standing at the worktop without a plate or napkin.

She had once been reassured by a senior politician – a woman – that the reason the poor could not manage on their state benefits was because 'they hadn't the aptitude to cook good, simple, nutritious meals.'

The Queen looked at her good, simple, nutritious broth bubbling in the pan and reached for another slice of bread and jam.

*

That evening, Prince Philip prowled around the bedroom muttering to himself. He stared out of the window. The street teemed with relations. He saw his wife and his sister-in-law coming out of his daughter-in-law's house. They crossed the road leading towards his mother-in-law's bungalow. He could see his son digging the front garden, *in the dark*, the bloody fool! Philip felt trapped by his relations. The buggers were everywhere. Anne, hanging curtains, helped by Peter and Zara. William and Harry yelling from inside a wrecked car. He felt like a beleaguered cowboy in the middle of a wagon train with the bloody Indians closing in.

He got back into bed. The vile broth, now cold, which his wife had earlier brought him, slopped over onto the silver tray and then onto the counterpane. He did nothing to stem the flow. He was too tired. He pulled the sheet over his head and wished himself somewhere else. Anywhere but here.

Winging It

The Yeoman Raven Master passed the White Tower, then retraced his steps. Something was wrong, he couldn't put his finger on it immediately. He stood still, the better to think. Japanese tourists took his photograph. A party of German adolescents sniggered at his silly hat. Americans asked if it was really true, that the Queen of England was living on a public housing project.

The Yeoman Raven Master remembered what was wrong at precisely the same time as a schoolgirl from Tokyo pressed the button on her Nikon. When the photograph was developed, it showed the Yeoman Raven Master with his mouth open in horror, his eyes wide with primeval fear.

The ravens had gone from the Tower: the kingdom would fall.

Thin on the Ground

It was Harry's first day at his new school. Marigold Road Junior. Charles stood outside the headmistress's office, wondering whether or not to go in. An argument of some kind was going on inside. He could hear raised female voices, but not what was being said.

Harry said, 'Eh up, Dad, what's goin' on?'

Charles yanked Harry's hand and said: 'Harry, for goodness' sake, speak properly.'

Harry said, 'If I speak proper I get my cowin' face smashed in.'

'By whom?' asked Charles, looking concerned.

'By *who*,' corrected Harry. 'By the kids in 'Ell Close, tha's who.'

Violet Toby came out of the headmistress's office, closely followed by the headmistress, Mrs Strickland.

Violet shouted, 'You lay a finger on one a my grandkids again and I'll 'ave you up, you 'ard-faced cow.'

Mrs Strickland did have rather a *determined* face, thought Charles. He felt the old familiar fear that schools always induced in him. He held even tighter onto Harry's hand – poor little blighter.

Mrs Strickland smiled icily at Charles and said: 'I'm sorry about that unfortunate scene. It was necessary to punish Chantelle Toby on Friday and her grandmother

Sue Townsend

rather took exception to it. Indeed, she seems to have brooded on it over the weekend.'

Charles said, 'Ah! Well, I hope it won't be necessary to punish Harry, he's quite a sensitive little chap.'

'No I ain't,' said Harry.

Charles winced at Harry's ungrammatical protestation and said, 'If you tell me which class Harry is to join, I'll take him along. . . .' A drop of water fell onto Charles's head. He wiped it away and, as he did so, felt another splash onto his hand.

'Oh dear, it's started to rain,' said Mrs Strickland. Charles looked up and saw water splashing down from cracks in the ceiling. A bell rang urgently throughout the school.

'Is that the fire alarm?' asked Charles.

'No, it's the rain alarm,' said Mrs Strickland. 'The bucket monitors will be along soon, excuse me.'

And sure enough, as Charles and Harry watched, children came from all directions and lined up outside Mrs Strickland's office. Mrs Strickland appeared at the door with a heap of plastic buckets which she doled out to the children, who took them and placed them strategically underneath the drips in the corridor. Other buckets were borne away into the classrooms. Charles was impressed with the calm efficiency of the operation. He remarked on it to Mrs Strickland.

'Oh, they're well practised,' she said, rebuffing the compliment. 'We've been waiting for our new roof for five years.'

'Oh dear,' said Charles. 'Er, have you tried fundraising?'

'Yes,' said Mrs Strickland, bitterly. 'We raised enough money to buy three dozen plastic buckets.'

Harry said in a piercing whisper, 'Dad, I gotta' havva' wee.'

Charles said to Mrs Strickland, 'Where, er, does one take him?'

'Across there,' said Mrs Strickland, pointing to the playground where rain was rapidly filling the potholes. 'He'll need this.'

She reached inside her office door and handed Harry an umbrella, decorated with the vapidly grinning face of Postman Pat.

'No inside lavatories?' said Charles in astonishment.

'No,' said Mrs Strickland.

They watched Harry struggling to open the umbrella before dashing through the rain towards a grim outbuilding where the lavatories were housed. Charles had offered to accompany his son, but Harry had shouted, 'Don't show me up, our Dad.'

Charles went into the headmistress's office and filled in a form registering Harry at Marigold Road Junior School. He was pleased to be told by Mrs Strickland that Harry qualified for free school dinners. When Harry had handed the dripping umbrella back to Mrs Strickland and she had replaced it in the umbrella stand inside her office, she led them along to Harry's classroom.

'Your teacher is Mr Newman,' she said to Harry.

They reached Mr Newman's classroom and Mrs Strickland knocked and walked in. Nobody saw or heard them enter. The children in the classroom were laughing too loudly at Mr Newman, who was doing a deadly accurate impression of the headmistress. Even Charles, whose acquaintance with Mrs Strickland was brief, could see that Mr Newman was an excellent mimic. He'd captured the jutting jaw, the brusque tones and the stooping posture perfectly. Only when the children fell quiet did Mr Newman turn and see his visitors.

'Ah!' he said to Mrs Strickland. 'You caught me doing my Quasimodo impression: we're doing French literature this morning.'

'*French* literature!' snapped Mrs Strickland. 'Those children have yet to learn any *English* literature.'

'That's because we haven't got any *books*,' said Mr Newman. 'I'm having to photocopy pages out of my own books – at my own expense.'

He bent down and shook Harry's hand, saying, 'I'm Mr Newman, your new teacher, and you're Harry, aren't you? Charmaine, look after Harry for today, will you?'

A plump little girl in gaudy bermuda shorts and a Terminator Two tee-shirt came to the front of the class and pulled Harry away from his father and towards a vacant chair next to her own.

'He's a free school dinner child!' announced Mrs Strickland, loudly. Mr Newman said quietly, 'They're *all* free school dinner children; he's among friends.'

Charles waved to Harry and left with Mrs Strickland. As they wove a path through the buckets in the corridor, Charles said, 'So, you're short of books, are you?'

'And paper and pencils and glue and paint and gym equipment and cutlery for the dining room and *staff*,' said Mrs Strickland. 'But apart from all that we're a very well-equipped school.' She added, 'Our parents are very supportive, but they haven't any money. There is a limit to how many raffle tickets they can buy and car boot sales they can attend. These are not the leafy suburbs, Mr Teck.'

Charles agreed; leaves were very thin on the ground on the Flowers Estate – even in autumn, he suspected.

Peas in a Pod

It was May Day. Charles shouted to Diana: 'Darling, close your eyes. I've got a surprise.'

Diana, who hadn't yet *opened* her eyes – it was only 6.30 in the morning, for goodness' sake – turned over in bed and faced the door. Charles came out of the bathroom and approached the bedside.

'Open your eyes.'

She opened one eye, then the other. He looked the same as ever, perhaps his hair was sleeker than usual . . . Then Charles turned his back and Diana gasped in dismay. He had a pony tail, only a very tiny one as yet, but even so . . . A bright red towelling band held his hair together at the nape of his neck. His ears were more prominent than ever.

'You look *fab*, darling.'

'Truly?'

'Yah, fabbo.'

'D'you think Mummy will like it?' Charles's face wrinkled into worry.

'Dunno. Your pa won't.'

'But you do?'

'It's fabuloso.'

'The beetroot is through and we've got our first blackbird sitting on its eggs.'

'Fabulous.'

Diana was getting used to these early morning gardening reports. He was up every morning at six, clumping around the garden in his wellingtons. She had *tried* to show interest, but gracious . . . She dreaded the autumn when he apparently expected her to preserve and pickle. He had asked her to start collecting empty jars, anticipating a glut of home grown produce. She got out of bed and reached for her silk robe.

'I'm so happy; are you?' he asked.

'Fabulously,' she lied.

'I mean,' said Charles, 'it proves that the garden is ecologically sound. Blackbirds won't . . .'

They heard Shadow crying through the party wall, followed by the creak of the bed springs as his mother got out of bed to give him his bottle of tea. Before going into the bathroom, Diana asked, 'Charles, I need to have my hair done. Could I have some money?'

Charles said, 'But I was planning to buy a bag of bonemeal this week.'

Through the wall Sharon shouted: 'I'll cut your 'air for you, Di. I used to be 'prentissed to an 'airdresser. Come round at ten.'

Charles said, 'The sound insulation in these houses is appalling. It's well, *non*-existent.'

Through the other party wall Diana and Charles heard Wilf Toby say to his wife, 'I 'ope Diana won't have 'er 'air cut too short.'

They heard the Tobys' headboard bang against the wall as Violet said, 'Oh shut your prattle,' and turned over in bed.

Then they went downstairs and searched the

cupboards for something to have for breakfast. Like the rest of their family in Hell Close they were sailing close to the wind financially. Indeed, they were dangerously near to being shipwrecked on the cruel rock of state benefits. Charles had filled in two sets of claim forms. Both times they had been returned with a covering letter explaining that they had been 'incorrectly completed'.

When the second form had arrived back, Diana had said: 'But I thought you were good at sums and English and stuff like that.'

Charles had thrown the letter across the kitchen and shouted, 'But they're not written in bloody English, are they? They're in officialese, and the sums are *impossible*.'

He sat down at the kitchen table to try again, but the computations were beyond him. What he did work out was that they could not claim Housing Benefit until their Income Support was known; and they could not claim Income Support until their Housing Benefit was assessed. And then there was Family Credit, which they were yet to benefit from, but which seemed to be included in the total sum. Charles was reminded of Alice in Wonderland as he struggled to make sense of it all. Like her, he was adrift in a surreal landscape. He received letters asking him to telephone but when he did nobody answered. He wrote letters but got no reply. There was nothing he could do but to return the third set of forms and wait for the state to give him the benefits it had promised. Meanwhile they lived precariously. They bartered and borrowed and owed fifty-three pounds, eighty-one pence to Victor Berryman, Food-U-R owner and philanthropist.

The milkman knocked at the door for his money. Diana looked around the kitchen and snatched a set of Wedgwood eggcups from the shelf. Charles followed her, carrying a silver apostle spoon. 'Ask him for a dozen eggs,' he said, pushing the spoon into her free hand.

Barry, the milkman, stood on the step keeping his eyes on his milk float. When the door opened he saw, with a sinking heart, that he was not going to be paid in cash, again.

Later that day, Charles was tying his broad bean canes together in the front garden, when Beverley Threadgold passed by, pushing her baby niece in an old high sprung perambulator. She was wearing a black PVC mini skirt, white high heels and a red blouson jacket. Her legs were blue with cold. Charles felt his stomach churn. He lost control of the canes and they fell to the ground with a clatter.

'Want some help?' asked Beverley.

Charles nodded, and Beverley came into the garden and helped him to gather the canes together. When Charles had arranged them wigwam fashion, Beverley held them together at the top and waited until Charles had tied them secure with green twine. She smells of cheap scent and cigarettes, thought Charles. I should find her repugnant. He cast around for something to say, anything would do. He must delay the moment of parting.

'When are we next in court?' he asked, though he knew perfectly well when it was.

'Nex' week,' said Beverley. 'I'm dreadin' it.'

46

He noticed that four of her back teeth were missing. He wanted to kiss her mouth. The sun came out and her split ends sparkled; he wanted to stroke her hair. She lit a cigarette and he, a vociferous anti-smoker, wanted to inhale her breath. It was madness, but he suspected that he had fallen in love with Beverley Threadgold. Either that or he was suffering from a virus that was affecting his brain – or at least his judgement. She was not only a commoner, she was common. As she started to move off Charles tried another delaying tactic. 'What an absolutely splendid-looking baby!' he said.

But baby Leslie was not, in truth, an attractive child. She lay on her back and sucked angrily on a large pink dummy and the pale blue eyes that stared up at the sky over Hell Close seemed old, like those of an old man disappointed by life. A rancid smell emanated from her. Her tiny clothes were not entirely clean. Beverley adjusted a fluorescent pink cellular blanket around Leslie's shoulders and took her foot off the brake of the pram.

Charles gabbled, 'Hasn't taken long to get to court, has it, our case?'

'Our' – what a precious word it was, signifying something shared with Beverley Threadgold!

'It's 'cos it's *you*,' said Beverley. 'They want you out of the way, don't they?'

'Do they?' said Charles.

'Yeah,' said Beverley. 'In the nick, where you can't do no harm.'

'Oh, but I won't go to *prison*,' said Charles. And he

laughed at the absurdity of the notion. After all, he was innocent. And this was still Britain, not some lawless banana republic ruled by a despot in sunglasses.

'They don't want you goin' round trying to get your mum back on the throne.'

'But it's the *last* thing I'd do,' protested Charles. 'I've never been so happy. I am, at this moment, Beverley, deliriously happy.'

Beverley dragged heavily on the last millimetre of her cigarette and then threw the burning filter into the gutter, where it joined many others. She looked at Charles's grey flannels and blazer and said: 'Warren Deacon's sellin' shell suits for ten pounds a throw, you ought to get one for your gardening. He's got some trainers an' all.'

Charles hung on to her every word. If Beverley advised it then he would find Warren Deacon, hunt him down and demand a shell suit – whatever it was. The baby started to cry and Beverley said, 'Ta-ra then,' and carried on down the Close. Charles noticed the blue veins behind her knees, he wanted to lick them. He was in love with Beverley Threadgold! He wanted to weep and to sing, to laugh and to shout. He watched her as she went through the barrier, he saw her spit with contemptuous accuracy at Chief Inspector Holyland's feet. What a woman!

Diana knocked on the window and mimed drinking out of a cup. Charles pretended not to know what she meant, forcing her to come to the front door and ask, 'Tea, darling?'

Charles said irritably, 'No, I'm sick of bloody tea. It's coming out of my effing pores.'

Diana said nothing, but her lip trembled and her eyes filled with water. Why was he being so horrid to her? She had done her best to make their frightful little house comfortable. She had learnt to cook his horrible macrobiotic food. She coped with the boys. She was even prepared to accept his silly pigtail. She had no fun. She never went out. She couldn't afford batteries for her radio, consequently she had no idea what records were in the charts. There was absolutely nothing to dress up for. Sharon had butchered her hair. She needed a professional manicure and pedicure. If she wasn't careful she would end up looking like Beverley Threadgold and then Charles would go *right* off her.

'Are you building wigwams for the boys?' she asked, coming out and touching the bean canes. Charles gave her a look of such withering contempt that she went back inside. She had cleaned the house and washed and ironed; the boys were out somewhere, there was nothing else to do. The only thing she had to look forward to was Charles's trial. She went upstairs and looked inside her wardrobe. What would she wear? She sorted through her clothes and selected shoes and a bag and was instantly comforted. When she was a little girl she had loved dressing-up games. She closed the wardrobe door and made a mental note to save her serious black suit for the last day of the trial – after all, Charles *could* go to prison.

Diana re-opened the wardrobe door. What should she wear for prison visiting?

Mechanicals

Spiggy was lying on Anne's floor in a pool of water at midnight. Anne was mopping up around him. She was wearing green wellingtons, jeans and a lumberjack's shirt. Her thick, blonde hair had escaped from the clutch of a tortoiseshell clip and cascaded down her back. Both of them were wet and dishevelled.

Anne had turned on the washing machine, gone out to visit her grandmother and returned to find the kitchen tiles floating in three inches of water. Spiggy had been sent for.

Anne asked: 'What did I do wrong?'

'Your hose is come loose,' said Spiggy, making an effort to sound the 'h'. 'Tha's all it is, but you done good! Ain't many women 'oo can plumb a washer in.'

'Thanks,' said Anne, pleased with the compliment. 'I must get my own tool set,' she said.

'Ain't yer 'usband got one?' asked Spiggy.

'I separated from my husband two years ago,' said Anne.

'Did you?' said Spiggy.

Anne was astonished, surely everyone in the English-speaking world knew her business, didn't they? Anne squeezed the mop into a galvanized bucket and asked, 'Don't you read the newspapers, Spiggy?'

'No point,' said Spiggy. 'I can't read.'

Anne said, 'Do you watch television, or listen to the radio?'

'No,' said Spiggy. 'They do my 'ead in.'

How refreshing it was to talk to somebody who had no preconceptions about her! Spiggy tightened the hose, then together they screwed the back plate onto the washer and pushed it in place under the formica worktop.

'Right,' said Spiggy. 'Owt else you need fixin'?'

'No,' said Anne. 'Anyway, it's very late.' Spiggy didn't take the hint. He sat down at the small kitchen table.

'*I'm* separated from *my* wife,' he said, suddenly feeling sorry for himself. 'Perhaps we can have a drink at the club one night, play a few games of pool?'

Spiggy put his arm on Anne's shoulder, but it was not a sexual move. It was the chummy gesture of one separated washing machine mechanic to another. Anne considered his proposition and Spiggy imagined making an entrance at the Working Men's Club with Princess Anne on his arm. That'd teach his mates to sneer about his size and shape. A lot of women liked small, fat men. Look at Bob Hoskins; he'd done all right.

Anne moved out from under Spiggy's dolphin-like arm and refilled his glass with Carlsberg. She glanced at herself in the mirror. Should she cut her hair? She'd had the same style for years. Wasn't it time for a change? Especially now, when she was at rock bottom: a single parent living in a council house, being wooed by a small, fat man at midnight.

'Yes, why not, Spiggs?' she said, surprising herself. 'I'll get a babysitter.' Spiggy could hardly believe his luck. He'd get a film for his camera and ask one of his mates to photograph him and Princess Anne chinking glasses together in celebration. He'd get the photo framed and give one to his mother. She'd be proud of him at last. He'd buy a new shirt; he had a tie some-where. He wouldn't make the mistake he made with most women: lunging at their bra straps on the first date, playing them his dirty joke cassette in the car. He'd go easy with her. She was a lady.

Reluctantly, he got to his feet. He rearranged his over-alls around his crotch. He had acquired a van. It stood at the kerb outside. An amateur sign-writer had written, 'L.A. SPIGGS, HIGH CLASS CARPET FITER' on the side. The previous owner was British Telecom, it stated in the log-book. This was the only legal document in his possession. He had no driving licence, insurance or road tax. He preferred to take his chance and, anyway, where was he going to get the money? I mean, after he'd forked out for the van? Legality was expensive and so was petrol.

'Right, I'm off,' Spiggy said. 'Gotta get my beauty sleep.'

Women liked you to make them laugh, he'd heard. Anne saw him to the door and shook his hand on the doorstep. She had to bend slightly to do so. But Spiggy felt ten feet tall as he slammed the door of his little yellow van and sped out of the Close with his exhaust pipe popping. Anne wondered if she should have told Spiggy that 'Fitter' was spelt with two t's.

The noise made by Spiggy's van woke Prince Philip and he began to whimper. The Queen cradled him in her arms. She would send for the doctor in the morning.

Lying Down on the Job

On Sunday morning, Doctor Potter, a young Australian with child-care problems, took Philip's hands in her own.

'Feeling crook, Mr Mountbatten? A bit low?'

The Queen hovered nervously at the end of the bed. She hoped Philip wouldn't be rude. He had been the cause of so many embarrassing incidents in the past.

'Of course I'm feeling bloody *low*. I'm lying down!' barked Philip, snatching his hands away.

'But you've been lying down for – what is it . . . ?'

The Queen answered, 'Weeks.' The doctor glanced at the titles of the books on the bedside table. *Prince Philip Speaks*, *The Wit of Prince Philip*, *More Wit of Prince Philip*, *Competition Carriage Driving*. She said, 'I didn't know you wrote books, Mr Mountbatten?'

'I used to do a lot of things before that bloody Barker ruined my life,' he replied.

Dr Potter examined Philip's eyes, throat, tongue and fingernails. She listened to his lungs and the beating of his heart. She made him sit on the side of the bed and tested his reflexes by tapping his knees with a shiny little hammer. She took his blood pressure. The Queen held her husband down whilst blood was removed from the vein inside the left elbow. The doctor used a spot of the blood to check his blood sugar level.

'Normal,' she said, throwing the test strip into the wastebin.

'So, may I ask if you have made a diagnosis yet, Doctor?' asked the Queen.

'Could be clinical depression,' said the doctor. 'Unless he's trying to swing a sickie. K'niver look at your pubes, Mr Mountbatten?' she asked, trying to undo the cords on his pyjama trousers.

Prince Philip shouted, 'Sod off!'

'K'ni ask you some questions, then?' she said.

'I can answer any questions you may have,' the Queen said.

'Nah, I need to know if his memory's crook. When were you born, Phil?' she asked cheerily.

'Born 10 June 1921 at Mon Repos, Corfu,' he replied mechanically, as though before a Court Martial.

The doctor laughed: 'Mon Repos? You're pulling my leg; that's Edna Everage's address, surely?'

'No,' said the Queen, tightening her lips. 'He's quite right. He was born in a house called Mon Repos.'

'Your ma's name, Phil?'

'Princess Anne of Battenburg.'

'Like the cake, eh? And your Pa?'

'Prince Andrew of Greece.'

'Brothers and sisters?'

'Sisters, four. Margarita, married to Gottfried, Prince Hohenlohe-Langenburg, Officer in German Army. Sophie, married Prince Christopher of Hesse, Luftwaffe pilot . . .'

'That's enough sisters, darling,' said the Queen, cutting in. Too many skeletons were coming dancing out of the cupboard – enough to supply a Busby Berkeley musical.

'Well, he's compos mentis,' said the doctor, scribbling on her prescription pad. 'Try him on these tranx, eh? I'll come back this arvo, take some urine. Can't stop now, I've got a list longer than a roo's tail.'

When they got to the bottom of the stairs, the doctor said, 'Trine clean him up, will ya? He stinks worse than a diseased dingo's den.'

The Queen said she would do her best, but the last time she had tried, he had thrown the wet sponge across the room. The doctor laughed: 'Funny how things turn out. I did my Duke of Edinburgh's Award y'know. Got a gold. Last time I saw your husband was in Adelaide. He was wearing a sharp suit and half a ton of pancake make-up on his face.' Doctor Potter hurried across the road. She had another house call to make in Hell Close. Poverty was hard on the human body.

POCKET PENGUINS

POCKET PENGUINS

36. **Muriel Spark** The Snobs
37. **Steven Pinker** Hotheads
38. **Tony Harrison** Under the Clock
39. **John Updike** Three Trips
40. **Will Self** Design Faults in the Volvo 760 Turbo
41. **H. G. Wells** The Country of the Blind
42. **Noam Chomsky** Doctrines and Visions
43. **Jamie Oliver** Something for the Weekend
44. **Virginia Woolf** Street Haunting
45. **Zadie Smith** Martha and Hanwell
46. **John Mortimer** The Scales of Justice
47. **F. Scott Fitzgerald** The Diamond as Big as the Ritz
48. **Roger McGough** The State of Poetry
49. **Ian Kershaw** Death in the Bunker
50. **Gabriel García Márquez** Seventeen Poisoned Englishmen
51. **Steven Runciman** The Assault on Jerusalem
52. **Sue Townsend** The Queen in Hell Close
53. **Primo Levi** Iron Potassium Nickel
54. **Alistair Cooke** Letters from Four Seasons
55. **William Boyd** Protobiography
56. **Robert Graves** Caligula
57. **Melissa Bank** The Worst Thing a Suburban Girl Could Imagine
58. **Truman Capote** My Side of the Matter
59. **David Lodge** Scenes of Academic Life
60. **Anton Chekhov** The Kiss
61. **Claire Tomalin** Young Bysshe
62. **David Cannadine** The Aristocratic Adventurer
63. **P. G. Wodehouse** Jeeves and the Impending Doom
64. **Franz Kafka** The Great Wall of China
65. **Dave Eggers** Short Short Stories
66. **Evelyn Waugh** The Coronation of Haile Selassie
67. **Pat Barker** War Talk
68. **Jonathan Coe** 9th & 13th
69. **John Steinbeck** Murder
70. **Alain de Botton** On Seeing and Noticing